It's Test Day, Tiger Turcotte

by

Pansie Hart Flood

pictures by

Amy Wummer

CAROLRHODA BOOKS, INC. / MINNEAPOLIS

Thanks to my son, Joey, who inspired me to write about Tiger Turcotte when his favorite books were all checked out of the library. To my readers, thanks for your continued support.

This book is available in two editions:
Library binding by Carolrhoda Books, Inc., a division of Lerner Publishing Group
Soft cover by First Avenue Editions, an imprint of Lerner Publishing Group
241 First Avenue North
Minneapolis, MN 55401 U.S.A.

Website address: www.lernerbooks.com

Library of Congress Cataloging-in-Publication Data

Flood, Pansie Hart.
It's Test Day, Tiger Turcotte / by Pansie Hart Flood ; illustrations by Amy Wummer.
p. cm.
Summary: Already so worried about the big second grade test that his stomach is upset, seven-year-old Tiger Turcotte, whose parents are Black, Meherrin Indian, and Hispanic, gets stuck on the question about race.
ISBN: 1-57505-056-0 (lib. bdg. : alk. paper)
ISBN: 1-57505-670-4 (pbk. : alk. paper)
[1. Race awareness—Fiction. 2. Racially mixed people—Fiction. 3. Test anxiety—Fiction. 4. Schools—Fiction.]
I. Wummer, Amy, ill. II. Title.
PZ7.F66185Ti 2004
[E]—dc21 2003008934

Manufactured in the United States of America
1 2 3 4 5 6 - JR - 09 08 07 06 05 04

With sincerity and joy,
I dedicate this book
to my family —P.F.

Dedicated to the open minds and hearts
of the Reading School District,
whose colorful population has flavored
and enriched our lives through
our own children —A.W.

CONTENTS

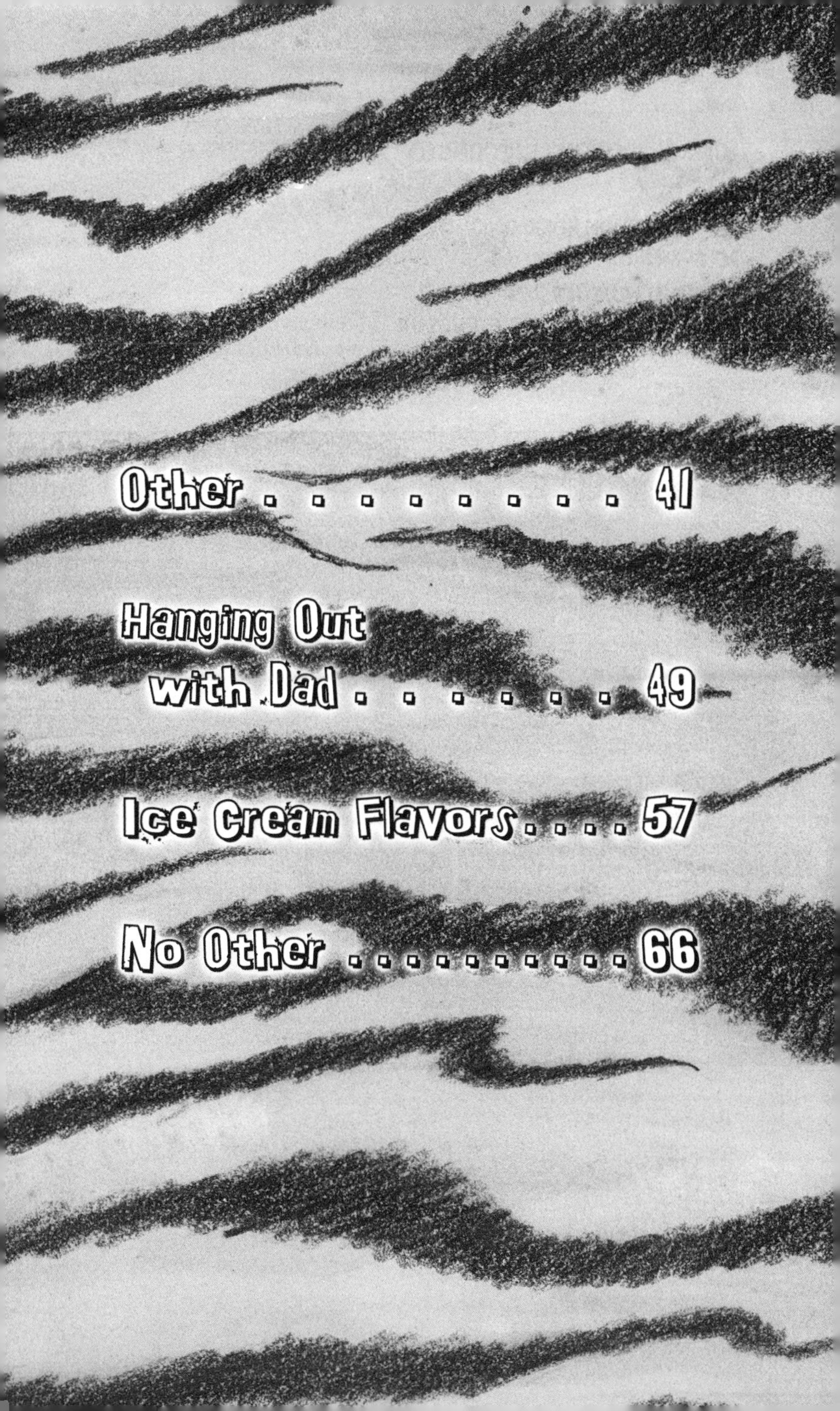

1 Lucky Pencils

BEEP, BEEP, BEEP!

My tiger alarm clock wouldn't let me sleep.

BEEP, BEEP—I hit the Keep-Sleeping button on the clock to stop the beeps.

My alarm clock makes two sounds. One goes beep, beep, beep. The other sounds like a giant tiger roaring. Like Rrrr!

My Nana Cruz gave me this tiger alarm clock for my birthday. That was last year when I was only six. I thought it would be neat to have a tiger wake me up. I was wrong.

The first morning, the Rrrr scared me so much, I fell out of bed. My mom and dad said I'd get used to the roaring. But I fell out of bed three mornings straight in a row. So we switched the clock to beep, beep, beep.

I still like listening to the clock roar. But only when I'm awake. And sometimes, I like to roar back. Rrrr!

Nana Cruz probably didn't know the tiger clock was so scary. She got it just because it was a tiger.

People like giving me tiger stuff because of my name, Tiger. My whole name is Tiger Turcotte. I turned seven on my birthday. It was July 17.

No, I'm not a tiger animal. I'm a boy. Now that I'm in second grade, I'm bigger. Last year, I was in first grade. First grade is for babies.

BEEP, BEEP, BEEP!

My tiger clock was beeping again. Mom says I only get to hit the Keep-Sleeping button once. So I had to get up.

I crawled out of bed like a real tiger. Then I remembered something very important.

"Oh, no! Today is the test! My first big test!"

I yelled 'cause I was nervous. I

was definitely moving up. In first grade, we didn't have any big tests.

My teacher said the test we were taking today was special. Why? 'Cause it would help us get ready for the real test coming up.

My stomach felt kinda funny at breakfast. Plus I had to rush so I wouldn't miss the bus.

Last year, I could take my time at breakfast. That's 'cause Mom was in college. She drove me to school every day. I liked that.

This year, Mom is a physical therapist. That means she helps people move their bodies after things like accidents happen to them. It also means I have to take the bus.

I tried to eat my cereal. But a ka-billion questions jumped around in my head.

"Mom?" I said.

"Yes, Tiger?"

"Do you think there will be a lot of math take-away questions on the test today?"

"I don't know, Tiger," Mom said. "There might be some."

Oh no, I thought. I'm good with adding. I get mixed up with subtracting.

"Mom?"

"Yes, Tiger?"

"What if I don't know the answers to any of the questions?"

"Tiger, there's no need to worry. Now hurry up," she said.

But I kept worrying.

"Mom?"

"Yes, Tiger?"

"I don't want to go back to first grade."

Finally, Mom stopped rushing. She smiled at me. She had a big piece of banana stuffed in her mouth.

"You're a very smart boy. I'm sure you'll do just fine. Okay?"

"Okay," I told her.

But I didn't want to take any chances.

After breakfast, I went to my bedroom. I opened the top drawer of my nightstand and pulled out three brand-new pencils.

These pencils are so cool. They're black with gold glittery stripes that glow in the dark.

I like playing with them like drumsticks. Sometimes I make up raps while I drum with my sticks.

These are lucky pencils. Why?

Because my best friends, Ted and Fred, gave them to me for my seventh birthday.

I tapped my pencils on the nightstand and rapped,

My two friends
Are Ted and Fred
They're kinda crazy
In their big, wacky heads

"Rrrr!" I roared. Not a good rhyme.

I shoved my lucky pencils in my pocket. I was ready for test day.

2

Rrrr!

"Tiger, you'd better get going or you'll miss the bus!" Mom called.

I looked out the window. Ted and Fred were already at the bus stop. Bus number 1619, my bus, was turning the corner.

"Wait for me!" I yelled as I flew out the front door.

"Run, Tiger!" yelled Ted and Fred.

I barely made it.

"Cuttin' it kinda close today," said my bus driver, Mr. Knight, as I climbed on the bus.

I flopped down into a seat next to Ted and Fred.

"Lucky you made it, Tiger," said Ted.

"Yeah," said Fred. "If you missed the bus, Ms. Bell woulda given you a tardy."

Ted and Fred are twins. They're in third grade. They told me all about tardies. And about Ms. Bell. Ms. Bell is the principal at my school. She is mean, very mean.

"Hey, guys," I said, "look what I got."

I pulled one of my lucky pencils out of my pocket. Just then, the bus turned a corner. My lucky pencil hit the floor and rolled away. I tried to find it, but it was gone.

"Oh nooo," I groaned.

"Too bad," said Ted and Fred.

Losing my pencil was even worse than getting a tardy. I only had two lucky pencils left.

My teacher, Ms. Newel, was standing at the door to my class when I got to school.

Sometimes Ms. Newel reminds me of Snow White. Her skin is very white, and her hair is very black. She's probably around sixty or seventy years old. Maybe even older.

"Good morning, Tiger," said Ms. Newel. "Are you ready for the test?"

"Yes, ma'am," I said. But really I was so scared, I could feel my heart beating in my shoes.

And when my ears heard the word *test,* my insides started to feel funny. I had to go.

I sat down and tried not to think about it. Then I tried holding my breath. Then I crossed my legs really tight. I was trying to get all the orange juice inside me from breakfast to go back up.

Ms. Newel said, "All right now, listen up! If you need to go . . . "

I raised my hand as high as I could. I bounced up and down in my seat like a frog.

Ms. Newel nodded her head. That meant I could go.

I ran into the bathroom so fast that I slid on some wet paper towels. I hit the stinky, nasty bathroom floor hard.

It hurt my butt really bad.

From the way it stung, I was sure my behind was red, blue, and purple.

I was not having a good morning at all. After I got up from the floor and made it into a stall, my zipper wanted to act up.

It would not move. My stupid zipper wouldn't unzip. I pulled up. I pulled down. I pulled to the right, then to the left.

"Rrrr!" I roared.

Finally, I got my zipper to work. I zipped it down as fast as I could, but it was too late. I had already started to go.

There's this guy named D'Andre in my class. The kids call him

Dumbo. Last year, D'Andre had an accident in his pants. He held it too long.

I remember Dumbo's—oops! I mean D'Andre's—pants like it was yesterday. After they dried, there was a huge shape right smack on the front. It looked like an elephant head with big elephant ears just like Dumbo's.

D'Andre had to walk around with Dumbo ears on his pants for the rest of the day.

Thank goodness I was wearing a pair of dark blue jeans. Why? 'Cause you couldn't see they were wet.

I tried walking as normal as I

could in wet underwear. It was awful and squishy when I sat down at my desk.

Inside, I secretly felt totally embarrassed. I tried taking my mind off the little bathroom accident. It was very hard, considering the fact that my butt was still very sore. The pain was way past ouchy.

3 Testing Has Begun

As soon as I sat down at my desk, Ms. Newel said, “Testing has begun. We’ll be taking part of the test today and part of it tomorrow.”

She had a big smile like she was happy we were taking a test.

Ms. White helped Ms. Newel pass out test booklets and answer sheets. Ms. White is a parent volunteer.

There's something kinda funny about Ms. White. Her name is White, but she is Black. That's like if your last name was Big and you were a little person.

When Ms. White passed out pencils, I didn't take one. Instead, I snuck my lucky pencils out of my pocket.

Phillip saw my pencils. "Ooo, cool! Can I have one?" he said.

"Shhh," I whispered. "You're gonna get me in trouble."

I looked down at my answer sheet. It had at least a thousand

tiny blue circles, like bubbles. Maybe more than a thousand. Maybe two thousand or five thousand.

Good thing I had my two lucky pencils left to fill in all those bubbles.

Ms. Newel went over a bunch of directions. She sounded like she was saying the same stuff over and over again.

"We got it already!" I wanted to yell out so bad. I felt like I was getting ready to take a test for the FBI or to work some place big like Disney World.

I was starting to get really bored. I wasn't the only one. Yaka was

playing with her charm bracelet. Tyrone was picking at his nose. (Which is a very disgusting thing to see, in my opinion.) Phillip had his chair tipped back so far, I thought he was gonna fall on top of me.

Usually that Donna Overton girl—yuck!—tells on Phillip when he does this. But Donna Overton was listening to every word Ms. Newel said. She looked like she was trying to win a contest or something.

Then I heard Ms. Newel say, "Make your mark heavy and dark

with your number two pencil. Fill in only one answer for each question."

Wait a minute! I panicked. What was a number two pencil? There was no number printed anywhere on my lucky pencils. What if they were number three pencils or number twenty-seven pencils?

What if my lucky pencils turned out to be unlucky? What if they made me get a zero on the test? I had to ask.

I held my lucky pencils straight up in the air over my head.

"What is it, Tiger?" Ms. Newel asked.

"I don't know what number my pencils are," I said.

I just knew Ms. Newel was gonna make me use a plain old boring yellow pencil.

"These are my lucky pencils," I told her.

Ms. Newel took one of my pencils and looked at it. I held my breath and crossed my fingers. "These should be okay," she finally said.

That was a close call. I was so glad, I tapped my pencils on my desk really soft and whispered,

My teacher Ms. Newel
Is a jewel

Hmm, not bad, I thought.

"We'll start with some easy questions," said Ms. Newel.

First, I had to fill in the bubbles that had the letters of my last name: T-U-R-C-O-T-T-E. Next, I bubbled in my first name, T-I-G-E-R. Then I had to bubble in my birth date, my grade, and my teacher's name. That was triple easy.

I bubbled in Male. Finally, I just had one more bubble left.

"Race? Umm . . . which race am I? Humm . . . "

The bubbles said White, Black, Hispanic, Asian, Native American and Other. "Rrrr . . . " I roared under my breath. This was definitely not easy. None of the answers were right.

I looked around to see if anybody else was having a problem. My luck, everybody seemed to be fine.

But I wasn't fine. Here I was in second grade and I didn't even know what I was!

4

The Race Question

I slowly raised my hand. How embarrassing. These were supposed to be the easy questions.

I got the attention of Ms. Black. Oops! I mean Ms. White. She walked over to my desk.

"I can't figure out which race bubble to fill in," I whispered.

"Oh?" she said. She looked at me

like I was some weirdo creature from outer space.

Then she hunched over and whispered in my ear, "Are you mixed? You look mixed. What color are your folks?"

I looked at her like she was crazy. "They're the same color I am," I whispered back.

Ms. White asked another stupid question. "Where were you born?"

"In a hospital," I said.

Ms. White stood up straight and looked down at me like she thought I was trying to be a smarty-pants. But the truth was, I really wasn't.

I raised my hand again to get the attention of my real teacher. Ms. Newel was sure to know the right answer. She is probably the oldest and the smartest teacher in our school.

Ms. Newel tippy-toed over to my desk. "Is there a problem?" she asked Ms. White.

They both stepped away from my desk. I knew why. It was so I couldn't hear what they were saying.

Then Ms. Newel stooped beside me. She smiled a very strange smile. She looked like something hurt.

"Your father is Black isn't he?" asked Ms. Newel.

"Yes, he is Black. He's also part Meherrin Indian," I told her.

"Well, what about your mother, Tiger? What is she?" Ms. Newel asked.

"My mom is from Costa Rica," I said.

"That means she's Hispanic," said Ms. Newel.

Ms. White came back over to my desk. "Tiger, I think you should bubble in Black," she said.

Then Ms. Newel said, "No! I think he should bubble Hispanic." She said that like she was mad at Ms. White and me.

"No! Excuse me, but I don't think Tiger's father would go for that," said Ms. White. She was talking kinda loud.

"Well, I don't think Tiger's mother would go along with your idea, either," said Ms. Newel in a very serious "I mean it!" kinda voice.

My head moved from right to left, from Ms. White to Ms. Newel.

I didn't know whether to be scared or excited. Something weird was going on between Ms. White and my teacher.

They went all the way out into the hall to talk things over. Donna Overton said really loud, "What did you do this time, Tiger?"

Just then the door opened wide. It was Ms. White. She came in, got her stuff, and left really fast.

The race question must be a really big deal, I thought. I felt bad about the whole thing. And I was worried too. Was I in trouble?

5

Other

When Ms. Newel came back in, she took a big breath and let it out real slow. Then she came over to my desk.

The next thing I heard made everything worse. Ms. Newel said, "Tiger, I think maybe you should fill in Other for now. It's the safest choice."

"Other?" I said. I felt my eyes open as wide as they would open.

What did Other mean? If I filled in the Other bubble, to me that was like saying I was weird or different from everybody else. That was like saying something was wrong with me.

I didn't feel like I was weird or different. I didn't feel like an Other.

I looked around. Everybody was already working on the test. If I didn't start soon, I'd get a zero for sure. I decided for myself that I had to leave the race bubble blank.

"What did you think about the test?" Ms. Newel asked when we were done.

"It was easy!" said Donna Overton. She had the nerve to look around the room with some silly smile like she was the smartest one.

I didn't say anything. I didn't even remember what was on the test. All I could think about was that empty bubble.

At recess, Phillip followed me out to the playground. "Hey, Tiger!" he said. "Wanna play tag?"

I scrunched up my face and rubbed my forehead like I had a headache.

"Nah, I'm not feeling too good," I fibbed.

Maybe it wasn't really a fib. I had so much important stuff on my mind, I was probably gonna get a headache.

I had something to figure out. I had to look for clues. Like a spy.

I hid behind a tree and peeked at the monkey bars. Donna Overton was hanging upside down.

Red hair. Freckles. Light skin. That's the White bubble, I decided.

A group of girls were playing double Dutch with jump ropes. I watched them out of the corner of my eye as I walked by. Collette and Rhonda were jumping together. Black, I decided.

Then I checked out the rope twirlers. Yaka was on one side. I knew she was Japanese. She musta bubbled Asian.

Patricia was on the other end of the ropes. What was she? I wondered.

Before I could figure it out Patricia said, "Hey, Tiger, wanna jump?"

I walked away fast like I didn't hear her. Was she crazy or what? Boys don't jump rope with a bunch of girls. Besides, spies work alone. And I had more work to do.

By the end of recess, I had almost everybody figured out. Everybody but me.

My skin is light, but I don't look White. My hair is light brown. It's curly on the top and straight on the sides.

My eyes are kinda small and very light brown. They almost match the color of my hair.

Grandma Turcotte says I have Turcotte cheekbones. "That Tiger

has got more Meherrin in him than his dad," she says.

I felt like the mixed-up kid. "Maybe I shoulda bubbled Other after all," I said.

6

Hanging Out with Dad

The longest school day in my whole life finally ended at 2:15. The bell rang. I grabbed my backpack and lined up at the door with the other car riders.

Dad was picking me up from school. It was his day off. My dad is a fireman. He works a few days.

Then he is off a few days.

"Hey, Tiger! How's my main man?" Dad said when he pulled up. "I need to do a small job at one of the duplexes. Then we'll have the rest of the afternoon to ourselves."

"Okay, Dad," I said.

My mom and dad own some duplexes. That's when two little houses are stuck together.

Taking care of those places is kinda like my dad's other job. Sometimes he pays me to help. I even get to do grown-up stuff like hammering and painting.

We stopped at Ms. Betty's house to fix a lock on her patio door.

Ms. Betty opened her front door and said, "Well, hello! Looka here at who's paying me a visit today!"

"Hi, Ms. Betty," I said.

"Y'all come on in," said Ms. Betty. "Tiger, you're growing like a weed. You must be at least a foot taller since the last time I saw you."

She says that every time she sees me. I don't mind, though. But if I grew as much as she said I did, I'd have to be about ten feet tall. Maybe taller.

"Hello, Ms. Betty. I hear you got yourself a broken lock," said my dad.

"Sure do. Come on back, I'll show you," said Ms. Betty.

Ms. Betty gave me a funny look while my dad was checking out the lock. Here it comes, I thought.

"Got any girlfriends to tell me about, Tiger?" she asked.

Ms. Betty says that every time she sees me too. Now that question I do mind.

"Ms. Betty, you know I'm too young to have a girlfriend," I said.

Ms. Betty laughed. Then she asked my dad, "What do you think? Can it be fixed?"

"No problem," Dad told her. "Tiger and I will have this finished before your soap opera goes off."

I usually like helping my dad. But today I couldn't stop thinking about that bubble I didn't fill in.

Finally I said, "Dad, Ms. Betty is White, right?"

Dad set down his screwdriver. "Yes, I think she's White. As far as I can tell."

I was surprised that Dad didn't sound for sure. "Can't you tell by looking at her?" I asked.

"Not really," said Dad. "You can't always tell a person's race by the way they look."

That just didn't make sense to me. Everyone I knew looked just like what they were. Everyone except me.

I sighed a big sigh. "But Dad," I said, "why don't I know about me? Everybody at school knows who they are. But I'm all mixed up.

"Well, I know *who* you are. You're Tiger Turcotte the third," Dad said. "We're done here. Let's go talk about this over some ice cream."

Ice Cream Flavors

Dad took me to Scoops, my favorite ice cream shop. I got two scoops of rainbow bubble gum. Dad got one scoop of butter pecan and one scoop of vanilla fudge swirl.

When we sat down, I spread out a napkin. I like to take all the little pieces of gum out of the ice cream and save them for later.

That's when my dad said, "Tiger, I must confess. Ms. Newel called me around lunchtime today."

Uh, oh, I thought.

But Dad said, "She explained everything that went on during testing. She felt really bad about all the confusion."

"Uh huh," I said.

For some reason, I was embarrassed to look at my dad. So I started counting my pieces of bubble gum. I had four blue ones, six pink ones, and one green one.

I could tell Dad was waiting for me to say something. So finally, I did.

"Dad, the test asked what I was, and I didn't know! Ms. Newel told

SCOOPS

us to fill in only one answer for each question, but I couldn't!"

My dad nodded his head like he understood.

"She wanted me to bubble Other. But I don't want to be an Other. Other is weird!"

Dad shook his head and said, "You're not weird, Tiger. There's nothing weird about being more than one race. You know what I am, don't you?"

"You're Black and you're Meherrin Indian too," I told him.

"Right," said Dad. "Do you think I'm weird?"

"Um, let's see . . . nah," I said.

Dad laughed. "Hey, Tiger," he

said, "how about a riddle?"

"Okay," I said.

"How is ice cream like people?"

I looked at my ice cream. It was cold. That wasn't like people. It was blue. That wasn't like any people I knew. It was melting all over my hand. What did that have to do with people?

"Um, 'cause you are what you eat?" I said.

"Well, that's true, but that's not the answer to the riddle," said Dad.

"Ice cream comes in many flavors, just like people come in many races. Sometimes flavors are

mixed together to create a different tasting ice cream."

"That's not a good riddle, Dad," I said.

"Maybe not," said Dad, "but it's important. No matter how many flavors of ice cream you mix together, you still have ice cream. Ice cream is ice cream and people are people. You just happen to be made of more than one flavor."

While my dad was talking, I put all my bubble gum in my mouth. There musta been twenty pieces.

I could tell that my dad really wanted me to understand that I'm not a weird person. But I couldn't talk with all the gum in my mouth,

so I just smiled as big as I could.

Dad laughed. "You are and will always be my main man, Tiger Turcotte. Look at you! You're wearing my dad's cheekbones."

Then I thought of something very important I had to ask. I took the gum out of my mouth and stuck it on top of my hand.

"Dad, I didn't answer the race question at all. Do you think Ms. Newel will be mad when she finds out? What if I have to take the whole test over again?"

Dad rubbed the curls on top of my head. "Everything is going to

be fine, Tiger. When did you become such a worry bug?"

I felt better about the whole race thing. But I had another problem. When I tried pulling the gum off

my hand, it stuck to everything.

Soon I had bubble gum all over my hands, all over the table, and even in my hair. It was a mess.

I did notice one thing, though, when we were cleaning it all up. All that blue and pink and green bubble gum had turned the same kinda gray color.

I guess even bubble gum is just bubble gum when you chew it all up.

8

No Other

"Today, we will take the second part of our practice test," said Ms. Newel the next day. "Before we get started, I'd like to know if anyone had a problem answering question number six about race."

I knew who she was talking about. She wasn't talking to everyone. She was talking to me.

I closed my eyes and put my head on the desk. "Why me? Why me?" I moaned.

I musta said it kind of loud 'cause the kids around me started to giggle.

"Tiger, are you not feeling well?" asked Ms. Newel.

"I'm okay," I said. But I kept my head on my desk.

Then I felt Ms. Newel's hand on my shoulder. In a soft voice she said, "Don't worry, Tiger. Everything is going to be okay."

I lifted up my head and opened my eyes. Three kids had their hands raised. I couldn't believe it.

I wasn't the only one.

"We'll talk about question six before we get started," Ms. Newel said. Then she passed out bubble sheets for the test.

"I found out we were using old answer sheets yesterday," Ms. Newel said. "I asked the testing center to send over some new ones for us to use today."

I looked at question six, the race question, on my answer sheet. Now it said White, Black, Hispanic, Asian, Native American, and Multiracial.

No Other.

"Multiracial has been added to the answer column for race," said Ms. Newel.

"That's weird," Phillip said. "What's Multiracial?"

"Would anyone like to answer Phillip's question?" Ms. Newel asked.

Yaka raised her hand. "My mom and dad told me it's like watercolors," she said. "You can paint with just one color, like red or blue. Or you can mix red and blue and get purple, and that's a color too. That's like me. I'm mixed with Black and Japanese, two races."

I was blown away. Yaka didn't look Black. I was sure she was just Japanese.

"Good example, Yaka," said Ms. Newel. "Can anyone think of other things that are mixed together to make one thing?"

"Mixed nuts," said Donna Overton.

"Vegetable soup," said D'Andre.

And of course I said, "Ice cream!"

I was finally ready to answer the race question. I wasn't scared anymore. I filled in the bubble that said Multiracial.

Then I did something extra special. I drew a line out to the side. Very carefully, I wrote Black. Then I wrote Meherrin Indian. Then I wrote Hispanic. And last, I wrote Rainbow Bubble Gum.

Nah, just joking. I erased that one.

That night, I finally made up a good rap. It goes like this . . .

There are no others
We're all sisters and brothers
I'm Tiger T., the man
Please understand me
If you can

Holla
Ice cream flavors
Vanilla, chocolate swirl
I'm proud of the races
Wrapped up in this whole world

Peace!
Rrrr . . .